IAN OLIO

MY LITTLE BOOK OF AIRPLANES

YOUNG EXPLORERS SERIES

For Kids
Ages 2-5

This book belongs To:

....

Today we are going to learn
about airplanes.

Since the beginning of time, people watched the birds and have wanted to fly. Birds make flying look easy, but they have feathers and light bones. People don't, but that didn't stop humans from wishing for flight.

The Chinese invented the kite in 400 A.D. In 1485 Leonardo Da Vinci drew pictures of flying machines. But the real history of flying started on December 17th, 1903. On that day Orville Wright and Wilbur, his brother made their dream come true.

Orville took to the sky in his first aircraft. The flight lasted only 12 seconds and finished after 36 meters. Despite that, Orville and Wilbur were happy that their dream of flying was now closer than ever.

From that day people did not stop designing new kinds of planes. They made a lot of mistakes but kept learning from them and thanks to that kept making better machines.

Today there is more than one type of airplane.

A passenger airplane is designed to hold many people and travel all over the world,

Jets are mostly used in the military.
They can reach speeds up to
2,500 kilometers per hour!

A helicopter is a type of a plane with huge blades on top of the body.

There are space shuttles which are made for traveling in outer space. They are between an airplane and a rocket.

Paper airplanes are made from paper and designed for fun.

How many people do you think the biggest airplane can transport?

An AirBus A380 can carry up to 840 passengers.

Isn't there just something cool about a vehicle which can defy the laws of gravity?

I hope you had fun learning about this short history of the airplane.

See you next time!

Made in the USA
Middletown, DE
22 March 2020